I0765552

# When My Right Is Wrong

Little Chickadee Teet Teet went to the
pond to eat.

He was very hungry and excited to eat
his favorite treat.

But when he got to the pond, all the water was gone.

"Who took the pond?" Teet Teet cried.

Teet Teet was very sad; he decided to go back inside.

"What's wrong?" Teet Teet, his friend Bits asked.

"Oh, it's just terrible, the pond is gone, and so is my food!"

"Oh no, don't you worry, Teet Teet, I know just what to do."

Bits took Teet Teet by the hand because he had the perfect plan. "Look at this food! There is plenty to eat. I'm sure here you'll find another great treat."

Teet Teet looked around at all the food. There were many treats, but none of them he wanted to pick. "Thank you, Bits, but this food isn't healthy; it will surely make me sick."

"Perhaps at first, your stomach might rumble, shriek, and grumble, but once you get used to it, you will be ok."
Bits began to eat and eat.

Teet Teet watched his friend stuff his mouth full.
Bits ate and ate till his face turned green.
"Bits!" Teet Teet yelled, "spit that food out; it's bad for you!"

Bits did not listen. He continued to eat, turning more and more green.
"This is not good," Teet Teet said to himself. "If he won't listen to me, maybe he will listen to our friend Lee."

"Lee! I need your help.
It's Bitz, he is eating very
bad treats! He is not
looking well."
Teet Teet looked up at
Lee, hoping to get help
for his friend. But Lee
had the same bad treat
in his hand.
"Oh no," Teet Teet said,
looking at the ground.
His hopeful smile turned
into a frown.

Lee ate his treat, just like Bits, and he too began to feel very sick.

"I know what to do," Teet Teet said with a glimmer of hope.

"I will go to Mrs. Beagle Beeks; everyone listens when she speaks.

Mrs. Beagle. I'm so glad to see you! My friends need your help. They are making themselves sick."

"You have come to the right place; I know just the trick."

"Hello, Lee and Bits, how do you do? Teet Teet brought me here to help you."
Bits looked up, confused, "We don't need help. I think you misunderstood. It's Teet Teet who needs help. He doesn't have any food. We offered him treats to pick, but he won't eat. He thinks they will make him sick."

"Oh, I see," Mrs. Beagle said.  "He has it all wrong. These treats aren't healthy, but you don't have to be healthy and strong."
Teet Teet saw Mrs. Beagle join his two friends. They were all eating bad treats, and all of them getting very, very sick.

Teet Teet sat down. Sadness filled his heart. *This is an emergency*, he thought to himself. I must get Councilman Bart.

'Councilman Bart. I have an emergency. My friends are in danger, and they won't listen to me!"

'Don't you worry, little chickadee, I know precisely what has to be done, so you and your friends can go back to having fun."

"Well, hello, Mrs. Beagle, Bits, and Lee. Teet Teet told me about your emergency."

"Oh, silly Teet Teet, he has got it all wrong. He thinks we need to be healthy and strong," said Bits.

"He wants us to stop eating our treats just because he has nothing to eat," said Lee.

"That's not true!" cried Teet Teet. "You do have to be careful about what you eat!"

"Now, now Teet Teet, let's think this through. It's very clear to me you do not understand food. These treats might make you sick, but what matters is that you enjoyed it."

"No, no, this is not right." Teet Teet tried to help his friends with all his might. But no one would listen, not even for a moment. He walked over to where the pond used to be and began to cry uncontrollably.

Teet Teet cried and cried and was soon very tired.
He laid down to take a nap.

Moments later . . . . .Teet Teet woke to the sounds of flap flap.

Teet Teet stood up and jumped for joy; the pond was back.

The pond was filled with healthy treats to eat!

Teet Teet began to eat happily.

He was surprised to look up and see Mrs. Beagle, Councilman Bart, Bits, and Lee.

Bits looked at his friend apologetically.

"Teet Teet, we were all wrong. We do need to be healthy and strong."

Teet Teet was happy to see his friends; joy filled his heart.

Everyone began to eat healthy treats: Mrs. Beagle, Lee, Bits, and even Councilmen Bart.

THE END

# OTHER WELLWAY BOOKS

- My Spot is Not
- Mrs. Betty Braker's Magical Bells
- Ben and Ben

WWW.WELLWAYKIDSTORIES.COM

www.ingramcontent.com/pod-product-compliance
Lightning Source LLC
Chambersburg PA
CBHW080812020826
48982CB00017B/940